Special Trees Around the World

Sally Cowan

Contents

Special Trees

Some kinds of trees are special.

Special trees grow in many places around the world.

Some of these special trees are very tall or quite **rare**.
Others look strange or beautiful.

Redwoods

The towering redwood trees grow in North America, in some forests near the sea.
They are the tallest trees in the world.

These enormous trees can live for a very long time.
Many of them are hundreds of years old, but some live to be more than 2000 years old.

Redwoods grow in North America, in the states of California and Oregon in the USA.

Redwood trees get water from fog that rolls in from the sea.

Redwood trees need a lot of water to grow.
It does not rain much in the forests
during summer,
but the trees have a special way
of getting enough water.
Their branches and leaves trap fog
that rolls in from the sea.
The water from the fog keeps the trees healthy.

In the past, many old redwood trees were cut down and the wood was used for making buildings.

Wollemi Pines

Wollemi pines (say: *Woll-am-eye*) are rare trees. There are only about 200 trees growing wild in a secret part of a rainforest in Australia.

Wollemi pines grow in this part of Australia.

In 1994, a hiker walked deep into the forest and noticed a group of strange-looking trees. They were tall, with lumpy, reddish-brown trunks. The branches were covered in stiff, thin leaves.

Scientists thought that Wollemi pines had died out with the dinosaurs. The scientists said it was a bit like finding a family of dinosaurs!

Wollemi pines have lumpy trunks.

In 2019, huge bushfires came close to burning the treasured trees down.

To save the trees, pilots flew special planes that dropped water on the fire.

The forest around the Wollemi pines was burned in bushfires.

Some firefighters were lowered to the ground from helicopters. They set up hoses to keep the trees wet.

The secret forest was saved.

A firefighter sets up a hose at a creek near the Wollemi pines.

Baobabs

Baobab trees (say: *bay-o-bab*) grow in parts of Africa, the Middle East and Australia.

These places have a hot dry season and a warm rainy season.

Baobab trees grow in these places.

This kind of baobab tree grows in Australia.

Baobab trees are often called bottle trees, because of the shape of their thick trunks. These trunks can **store** a lot of water. The trees need the water in their trunks to stay alive during the dry season.

This kind of baobab tree grows in Africa.

People who live in these hot places
can get water and food from baobab trees.

In the wet season, the trees grow leaves and fruit.
The large fruit is a healthy food,
and the leaves can be eaten, too.

The fruit from baobab trees is healthy to eat.

Some very old baobab trees are hollow inside, and can be used for shelter.

Dragon's Blood Trees

Dragon's blood trees grow wild on some dry, rocky islands in Yemen in the Middle East.

Dragon's blood trees grow on four small islands in Yemen.

These rare trees have bright red **sap**. People used to think this sap was dragon's blood.

In one old story that people told, a dragon and an elephant had a fight. The dragon got hurt. Soon after, a strange tree appeared with lumpy bark and spiky leaves. It grew in the place where the dragon's blood had gone into the ground.

The sap from the dragon's blood tree has been used to make medicines for hundreds of years.

The sap of dragon's blood trees is bright red

Coconut Palms

Coconut palms grow wild on **tropical** islands in the Pacific Ocean. These trees have tall, thin trunks that bend with the wind. The leaves and coconuts grow at the top of the tree.

Coconut palms grow on many tropical islands.

Coconut palms have a special way of spreading from island to island. If a coconut falls into the sea, it can float in the water for many years and go a long way.

When a coconut washes up on the beach of another island, a new palm tree can grow from it.

Cherry Blossom Trees

Cherry blossom trees grow wild
in some forests in Asia.
But people have planted the trees
in cities all over the world,
because they are so beautiful.

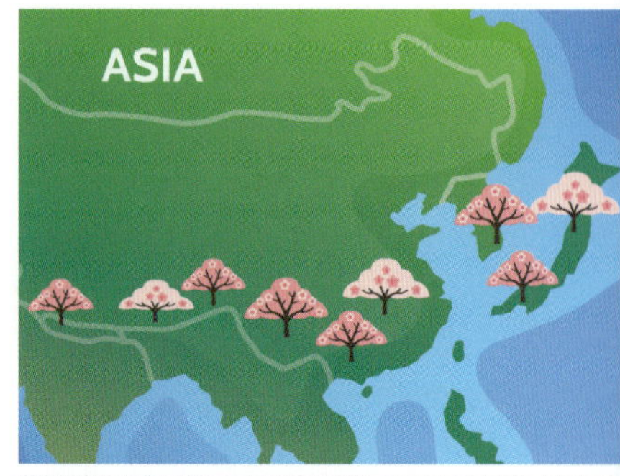

Cherry blossom trees grow wild in Asia.

In spring, lots of tiny
pink flowers appear.
They make people
feel excited and happy
after a long, cold winter.

For hundreds of years, people have painted pictures of cherry blossom trees. They have sung songs about them, too.

This artwork is by Kitagawa Utamaro.

A Wonderful World

Special trees grow in forests
or in hot, dry places.
They grow on tropical islands
or in busy cities.

These special trees make the world
a wonderful place.

Glossary

rare (*adjective*) hardly ever found

sap (*noun*) the sticky liquid inside trees and plants

store (*verb*) to keep something to use when it is needed

tropical (*adjective*) very hot but not dry; often rainy or humid